hic,
hic,
hic

To Kiko
—M. C.

To Susan—my online savvy shopper who found
me the best bones
—S. D. S.

ISBN 0-439-47913-4

Text copyright © 2002 by Margery Cuyler. Illustrations copyright
© 2002 by S. D. Schindler. All rights reserved. Published by
Scholastic Inc., 557 Broadway, New York, NY 10012, by arrange-
ment with Margaret K. McElderry Books, Simon & Schuster
Children's Publishing Division. SCHOLASTIC and associated logos
are trademarks and/or registered trademarks of Scholastic Inc.

12 11 10 9 8 7 6 5 4 3 2 1   3 4 5 6 7 8/0

Printed in the U.S.A.   09

First Scholastic printing, September 2003

Book design by Kristin Smith

The text of this book is set in Caxton.

The illustrations are rendered in gouache, watercolor, and ink.

SKeLeToN hiCcups

by margery cuyler

illustrated by S. d. schindler

SCHOLASTIC INC.

New York Toronto London Auckland Sydney
Mexico City New Delhi Hong Kong Buenos Aires

Skeleton woke up.

hic,
hic,
hic

Had the hiccups.   hic, hic, hic

Took a shower.

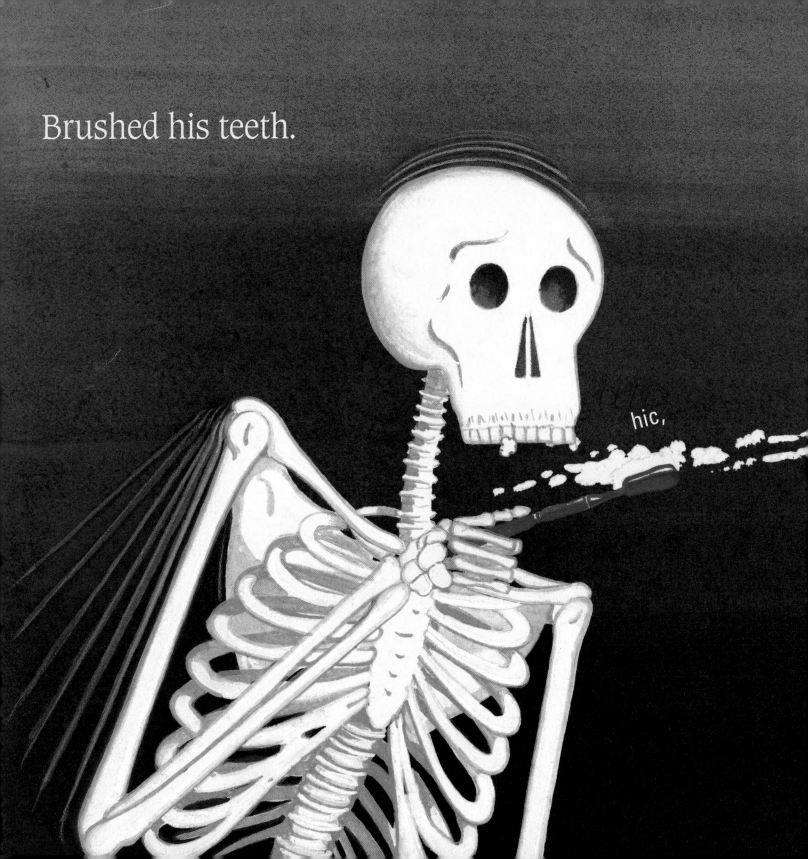

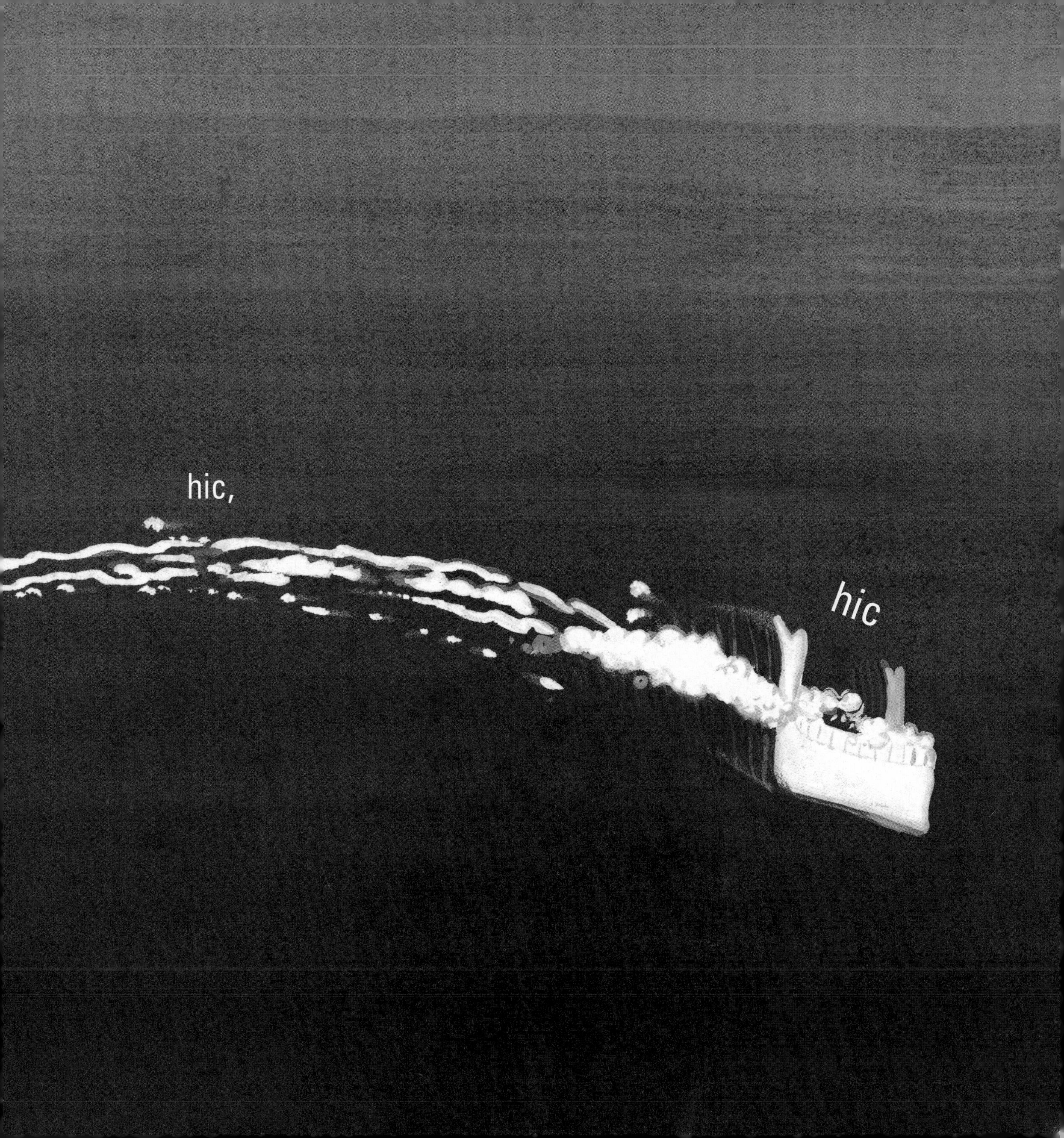
hic,
hic

Polished his bones.

hic, hic, hic

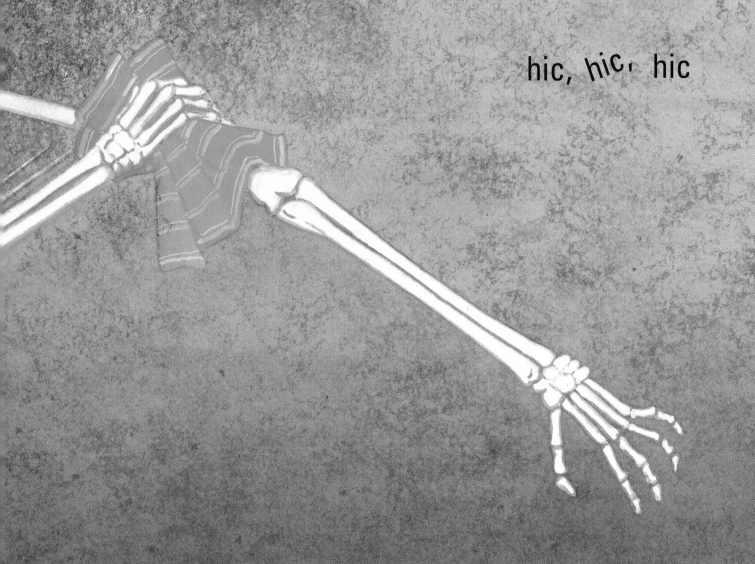

Carved a pumpkin.

Raked some leaves.

hic,

hic,

hic

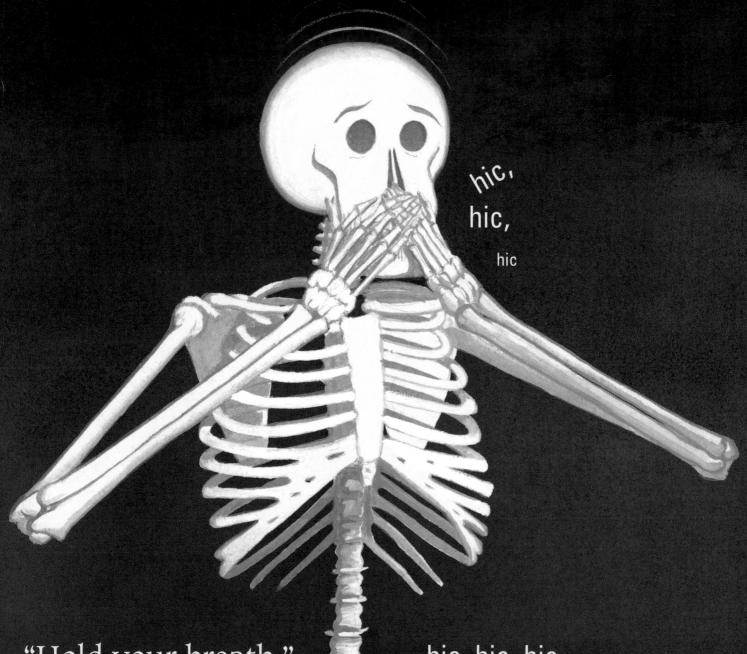

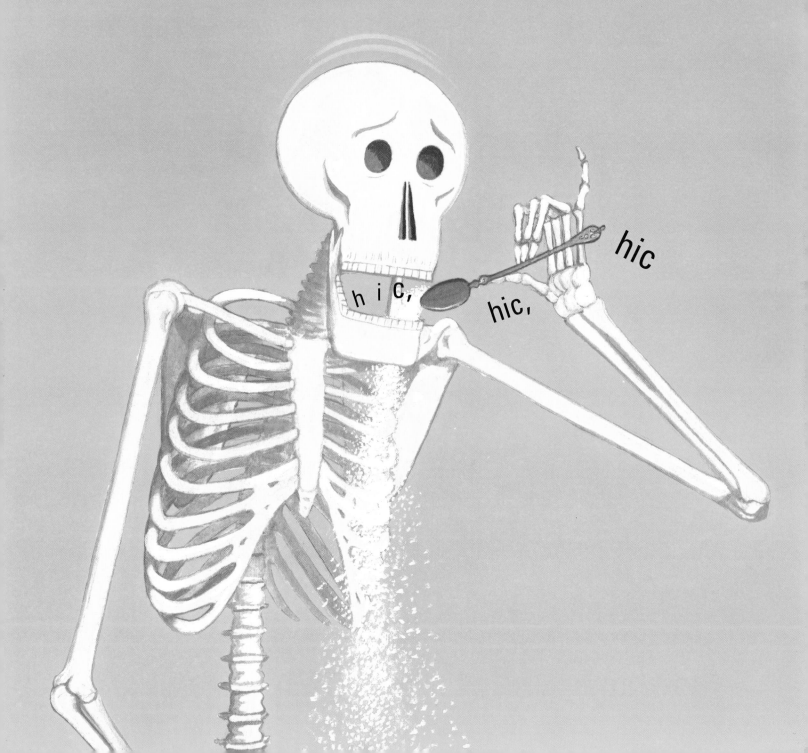

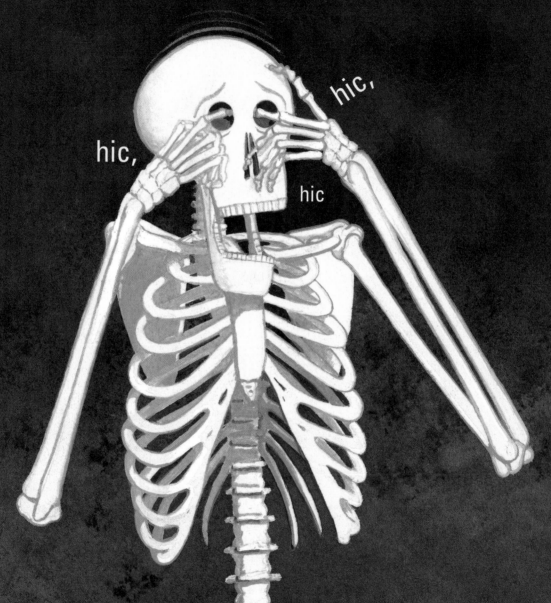

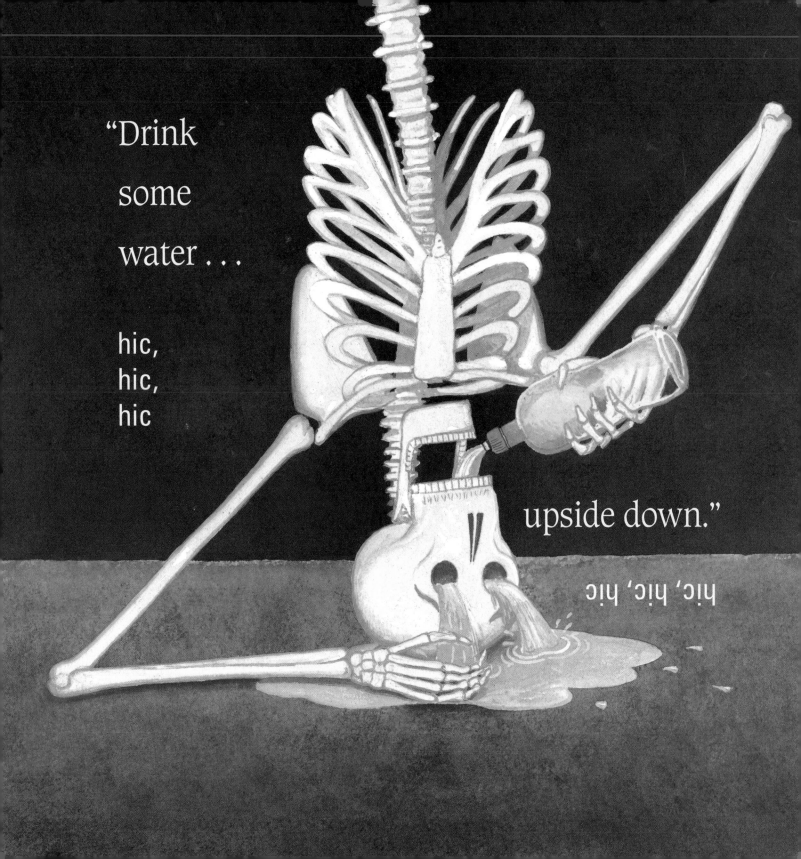

Ghost made a face.

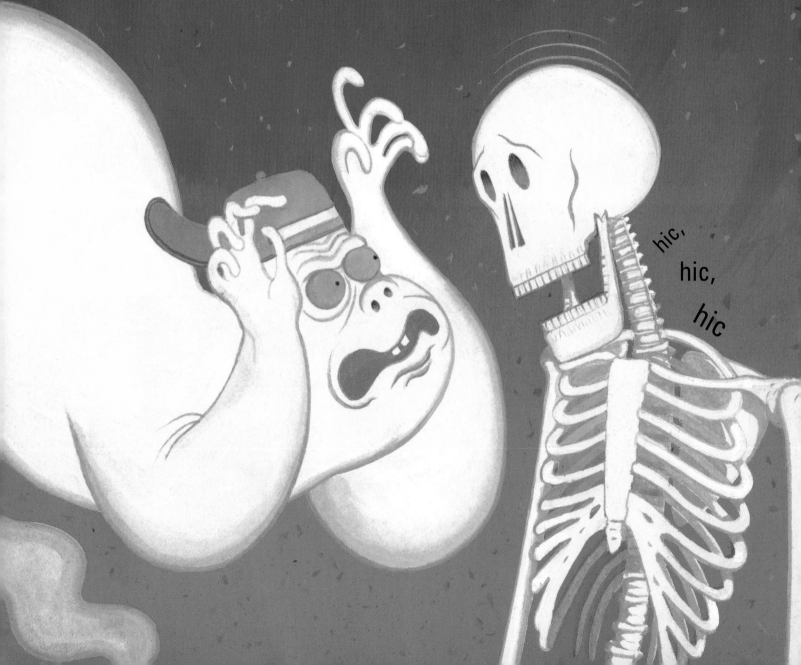

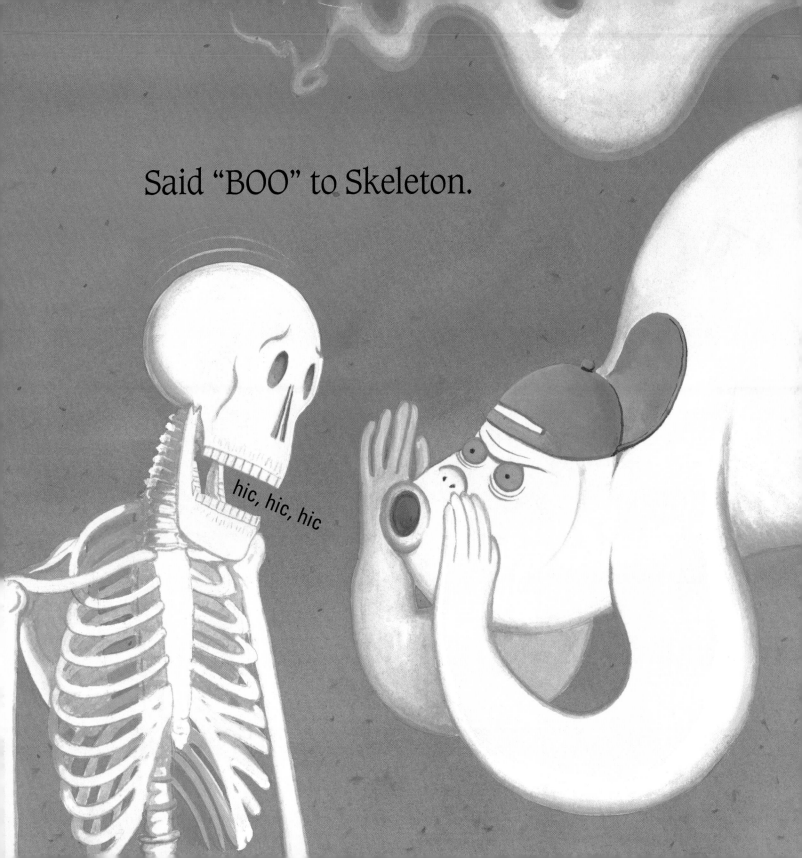

But nothing worked.

hic, hic, hic

The hiccups
stayed.

hic,
hic,
hic

Then Ghost got smart.

hic, hic, hic

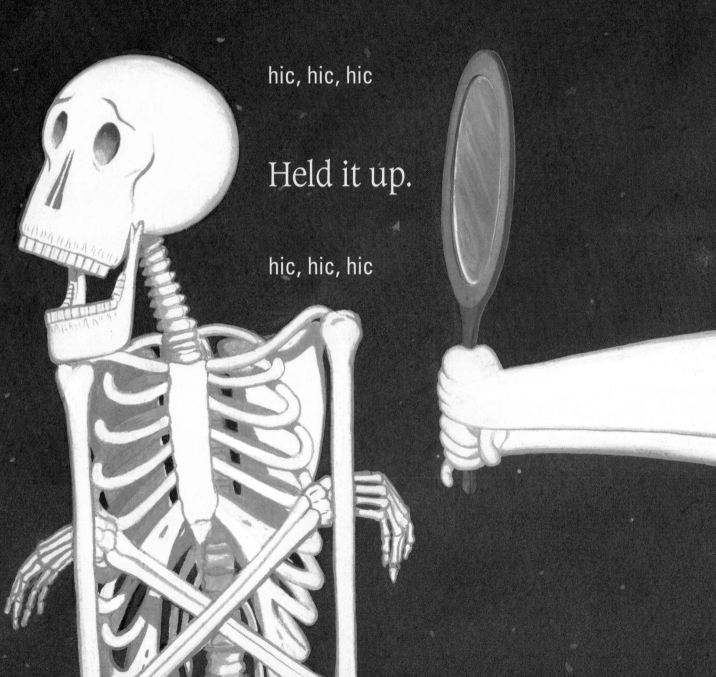

Found a mirror.

hic, hic, hic

Held it up.

hic, hic, hic

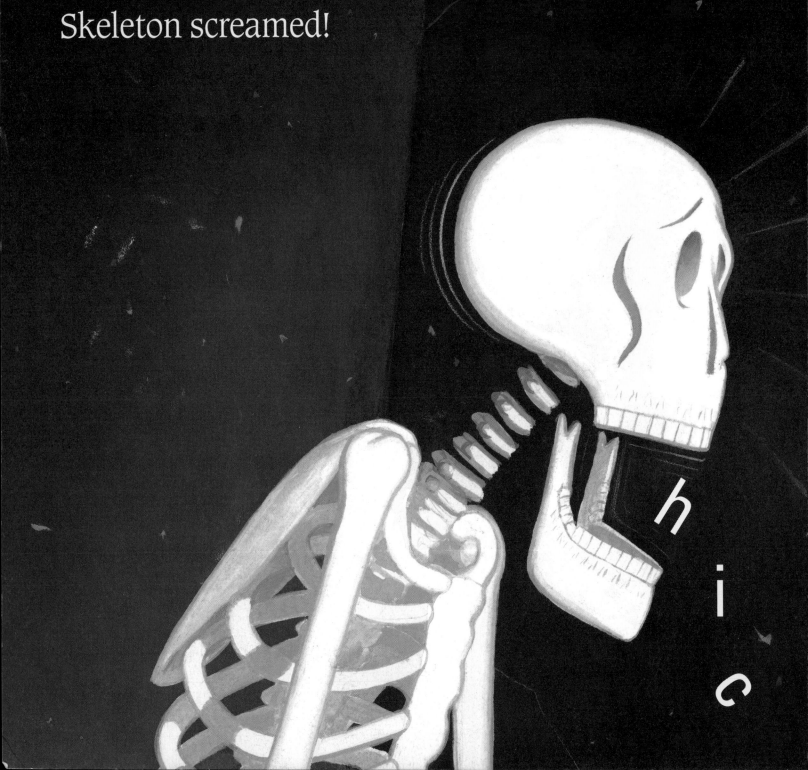

Skeleton screamed!

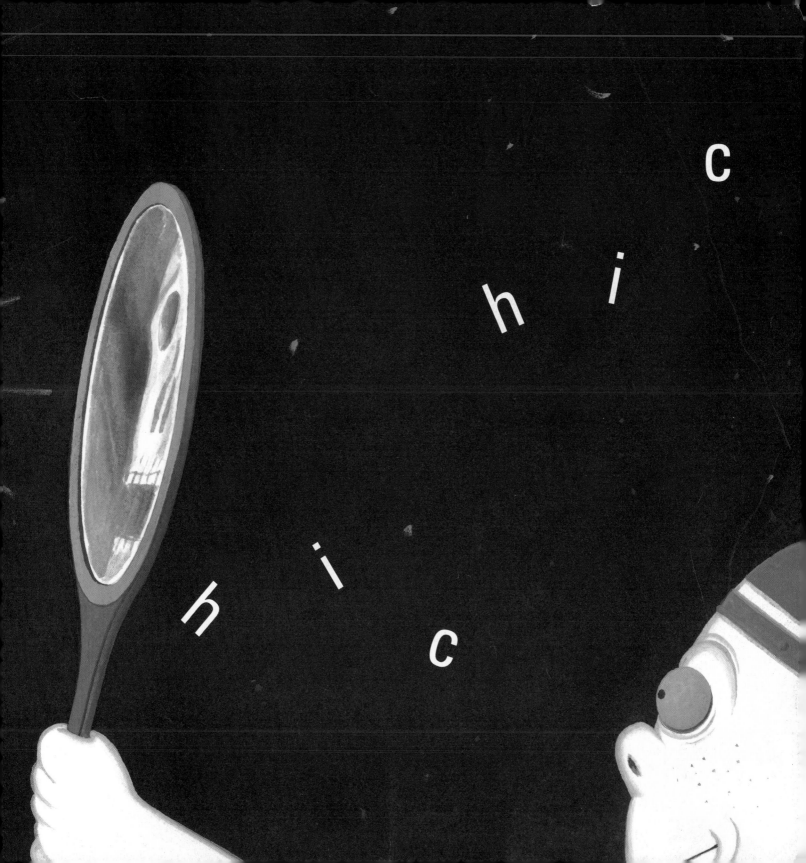

The hiccups left.

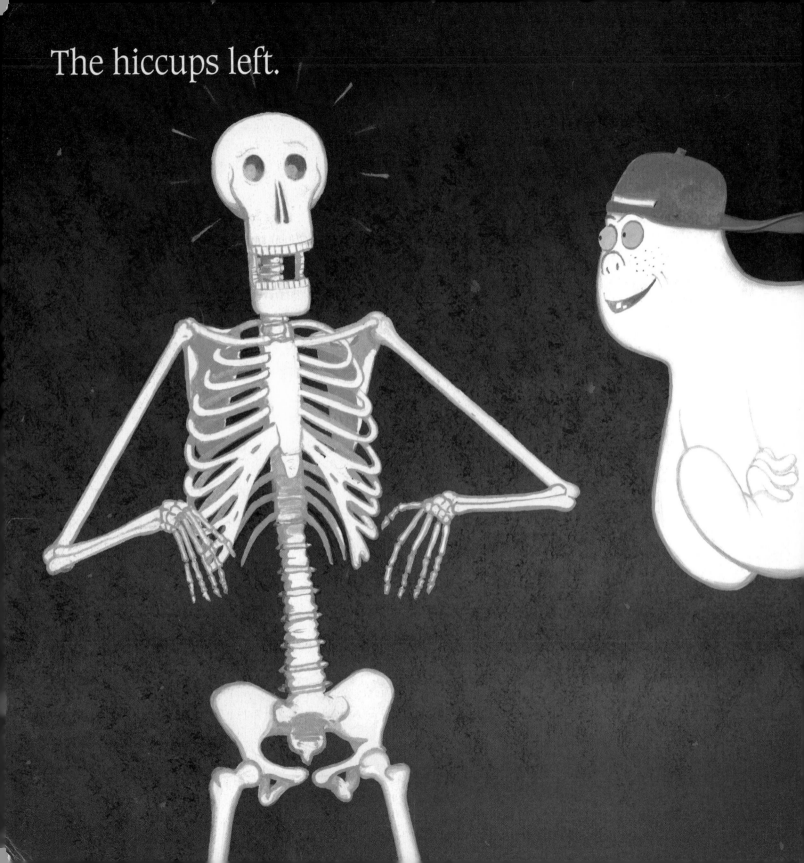

hic, hic, hic